There's a
Monster
IN YOUR BOOK

Written by TOM FLETCHER

Illustrated by GREG ABBOTT

PUFFIN

For Miss Summer Rae, the newest monster in the family! – T.F.

For Roger – G.A.

PUFFIN BOOKS

UK | USA | Canada | Ireland | Australia | India | New Zealand | South Africa

Puffin Books is part of the Penguin Random House group of companies whose
addresses can be found at global.penguinrandomhouse.com.

www.penguin.co.uk
www.puffin.co.uk
www.ladybird.co.uk

Penguin
Random House
UK

First published 2017

005

Copyright © Tom Fletcher, 2017
Illustrated by Greg Abbott

The moral right of the author has been asserted

Printed in Italy

A CIP catalogue record for this book is available from the British Library

ISBN: 978-0-141-37609-7

All correspondence to:
Puffin Books, Penguin Random House Children's, 80 Strand, London WC2R 0RL

OH NO!
There's a monster in your book!

Let's try to get him out.

shake the book

and turn the page . . .

Nice try – that knocked him over, but he's
STILL IN YOUR BOOK!

Tickle

his feet and turn the page . . .

That didn't work – he's just laughing and he's
STILL IN YOUR BOOK!

Try blowing him away.

BLOOW

really hard and turn the page . . .

That's better – now he's far away, but he's
STILL IN YOUR BOOK!

TILT the book to the left . . .

Now he's over here, but he's . . .

STILL IN YOUR BOOK!

TILT the book to the right . . .

He's hanging on!

What a naughty little monster!

Give the book a good

wiggle...

OK, now he's back over there.
But there's **STILL** a monster in your book!

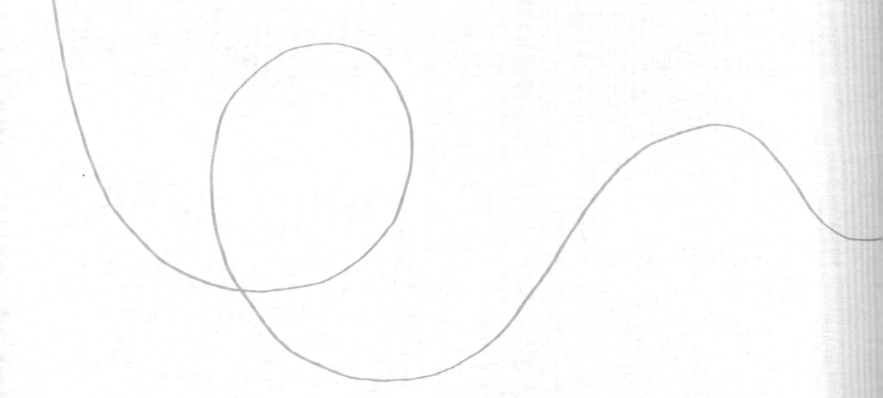

Try **spinning** the book round and round . . .

Look! He's dizzy!

Quick, make a

LOUD

noise . . .

It's working! He's running away!

Make that noise again, but . . .

HE'S GONE!

There **ISN'T** a monster in your book any more . . .

Now he's in your room!

Quickly, call him back . . .
Monster, come back!

Look! Here he is!

He's coming back.

Keep calling him . . .

Monster!

Come here, little monster!

PHEW!

He's back in your book.

You don't want a monster loose in your room!
This book is probably the best place to keep him.

Monster, you can stay here in this book!

Stroke Monster's head and say goodnight . . .

Goodnight, Monster.

SHHH!
Look! He's fast asleep.

Gently close the book so he doesn't wake up.